Amateur Dreams

Reaching New Heights

Alexis
Minnich

outskirts
press

Amateur Dreams
Reaching New Heights
All Rights Reserved.
Copyright © 2024 Alexis Minnich
v2.0

This is a work of fiction. Names, characters, businesses, places, events, locales, and incidents are either the products of the author's imagination or used in a fictitious manner. Any resemblance to actual persons, living or dead, or actual events is purely coincidental.

The opinions expressed in this manuscript are solely the opinions of the author and do not represent the opinions or thoughts of the publisher. The author has represented and warranted full ownership and/or legal right to publish all the materials in this book.

This book may not be reproduced, transmitted, or stored in whole or in part by any means, including graphic, electronic, or mechanical without the express written consent of the publisher except in the case of brief quotations embodied in critical articles and reviews.

Outskirts Press, Inc.
http://www.outskirtspress.com

ISBN: 978-1-9772-6707-8

Cover Photo © 2024 www.gettyimages.com. All rights reserved - used with permission.

Outskirts Press and the "OP" logo are trademarks belonging to Outskirts Press, Inc.

PRINTED IN THE UNITED STATES OF AMERICA

DEDICATION

This book is dedicated to my mother, Susan, and my trainer, Michelle. Without the two of you there would be no Jack and Alexis.

To all those adult amateur equestrians out there, those of us who are slightly older, don't bounce back as easily, may not have the fanciest horse, work countless hours to pay for our show entry fees, spend hours and hours at the barn with our horse, and have so much love and respect for this amazing sport of ours …, this book is for you.

And to Jack, my amazing horse. I am on this journey because of you.

ACKNOWLEDGMENTS

Writing a book is harder than I thought. Seeing it come to fruition and my journey laid out for everyone to read is more humbling and rewarding than I ever could have imagined. None of this would have been possible without the continuing support and encouragement I received from my family and friends.

A very special thank you to my equestrian family, the ones I could lean on when the times got tough, when I wasn't sure where my road with Jack was headed or when I just needed someone to talk to.

To all the people I sent endless copies of my book to throughout this process looking for thoughts and feedback, good or bad, thank you. Your opinions are the ones that meant the most to me, and this book would not have been possible without your help.

The those friends that I've known since grade school who listen to me rattle on for hours about Jack and riding, even though they really have no idea what I am talking about, the family members who congratulate me and spend hours and hours at horse shows bored out of their minds when I ride for only ten minutes, and the coworkers who notice when I've put a new photo in my office and don't mind when I have to leave early "because my horse needs me."

To my niece Khloe, the first person I shared my story with and the one who encouraged me to publish it, thank you. As she is a future equestrian star herself, I hope this book continues to fuel her love and passion for horses as her faith in me fueled my courage to publish.

To my publishing team at Outskirts Press. Working with you was such a pleasure from beginning to end. You helped turn my little story into this beautiful piece of art. Thank you.

Writing this story about my personal experience has been surreal, enlightening, and an incredibly enjoyable and fulfilling experience.

INTRODUCTION

*H*ave you ever had a passion for something? Something that touched your very soul? That is what horses are for me. They are magnificent in every way. They challenge us, understand us, love us unconditionally, and are some of the most majestic creatures on the planet.

Equestrians for the most part all have a similar journey. You start learning to ride on the safe, older school horse, first being taught how to groom them and what each piece of their tack is and what it is used for. But as you grow and advance you get the chance to really bond with the horses. You must, because you can't just ask 1,200-pound animals to jump three-foot fences without some level of trust between the two of you.

If you are lucky enough, your journey moves into ownership, and that is the ultimate horse lover's dream, to have a horse of your very own. That process can be the most incredible life-changing experience or it can be one of the most challenging. Both are no less rewarding in the end.

What has my journey been like? I would say that mine has been a combination of both. How do you decide which horse is right for you? How do you decide when the horse you have spent so much time on might not be the one for you? When is enough, enough? What does it feel like when everything finally comes together? Adult amateur equestrians rely on the advice of those around us. Our community is like our rock, and the opinions of those in our community are very important.

Our story has been riddled with many challenges, but as you will learn, we have also been blessed with many rewarding moments. What ultimately will happen to Jack and me? Only time will tell, but for now here's the tale of us—our tale from track to team.

WELCOME HOME

"*Ve con dodo.*" This quote is from a book I read this past summer, and it stuck with me. "Let it ride." This has been my motto for the past couple of months. As an equestrian you come to expect times of great highs but also periods of uncertainty and doubt. I have been riding horses for more than half my life. Riding horses is a freeing, humbling, and therapeutic experience. When I am in the saddle riding horses and jumping fences, I feel like I am flying, like nothing can touch me and all the problems of the day just melt away. Horses do that for me and for anyone lucky enough to have them in their lives. In a way they almost understand us better than we understand ourselves.

I didn't buy my first horse until I was older. I was fortunate enough to ride at a barn that had some of the most amazing lesson horses. The first horse I owned was actually a lesson horse at the barn where I was taking lessons, Chasing Dreams. His name was Irish, and he was a big, beautiful grey with the sweetest disposition. When I was given the chance to buy him, I couldn't say no; he and I had an amazing connection. Unfortunately horses don't live forever, and I lost him a little over five years ago. He was older, but we had many amazing rides in our time together and was wonderful with my niece and nephews when they rode him.

I didn't want to be without my own horse forever, and the time had come to start the search for my next "Irish." What did I want? Well, I had it in my mind that I was going to buy a big, beautiful dark bay with four white socks. What stole my heart? The complete opposite: an untrained, fresh off-the-track little baby chestnut horse named Jack, which I guess is fitting, both horse names being types of whiskey. I should have known I'd stick with the theme.

Jack was what I considered my "bucket list" horse. For as long as I could remember I wanted to help retrain an off-the-track Thoroughbred, or OTTB, as we call them in the horse world. Although he wasn't what I went looking for when I started my search, he turned out to be exactly what I needed. I consider myself a good rider, but I had never worked with OTTBs before, and they require a certain touch when you restart them. I was lucky though; I have a trainer who specializes in them and was supportive from the very beginning. She went with me when I did my trial ride on Jack and said, "If you're going to do it, he seems like a good one to go with." And with that, my journey as an OTTB owner and trainer began.

LEARNING CURVE

*W*hen I first brought Jack home, we decided to let my trainer work with him for the first full week. I had the option to basically hand him over to her fulltime for a while, but I really wanted to be hands-on with his training.

Those first few months with Jack went as I expected, textbook, as my trainer said they would. He was learning to use his body differently and we were working on building our relationship. He was putting on muscle and growing quite rapidly. He was no longer that scrawny baby Thoroughbred I purchased, He was turning into a gorgeous, well-built, tall horse.

It wasn't that long after I first bought Jack that my trainer and I felt strongly enough in his training to send him to his first show. My trainer would be the one showing him his first time out, and this would be a major step in his development into a hunter/jumper.

Jack took it all in stride, the trailer ride over to Harmony Acres, walking around the arena before the show, even learning how to navigate the intense show atmosphere. I was proud of him. Jayne, the trainer, really had him looking like a seasoned pro out there. I couldn't wait for the next show and the chance to get out there myself.

And that's exactly what happened. The next show Jayne felt Jack and I were doing well enough as a team to try our hands at the walk trot class. No flat classes yet, jumping only, and I was ecstatic. I thought this was it, the first step to our 3' career. We did very well in our first show, and I made sure to commemorate the occasion with pictures. I mean you get to have your first-ever horse show together only once.

Attitudes Change

It was around the sixth month that things really started to change. Jack became difficult to handle sometimes and ended up spending time at the vet for ulcers. He would literally run away with me, honestly, I didn't know horses ran that fast and bucked for no reason. We did all the things that a responsible horse owner should do when your horse acts up, we had the vet check him for pain, illness, etc., double checked all his tack, and I even handed him over to my trainer for a few weeks to work with him.

There was nothing physically wrong with him, and I think I took those first six months for granted, getting complacent. I almost forgot that he was still a baby and an ex-racehorse in training. Things had started off almost too perfectly, but we started to realize that Jack seemed to have a reactionary nature that we weren't expecting, and I am not the quietest rider. Those two things created an uncomfortable situation.

It was during this time that I ended up injured, one of many since Jack and I became a team, but this injury sidelined me for a few weeks. On what seemed like a normal lesson night when Jack and I were working on jumping, this was still new for us at this point, we came off a fence and something set him off. To this day I am not sure what it was. He started bucking like he was a bronc horse at a rodeo. I couldn't maintain my seat and ended up being thrown against the wall.

I panicked and yelled for my trainer. Jack stood over me, as if aware of what had just happened. "Jayne, Jayne, I can't feel my legs. I can't feel my legs." I have replayed that moment in my head over and over. The sensation was completely gone from my waist down. "This is it," I thought. "This is where it all ends."

I remember Jayne running across the arena. "Try and relax; breathe. You are in shock. Breathe, breathe."

I just kept hearing her tell me to breathe and not move.

After what I thought was an hour but was actually just about five minutes, all the feeling in my legs returned, pain pulsating all the way up my back. This injury hurt; it would be the one and only time I wouldn't get back in the saddle. No matter how bad I wanted to, I just couldn't. Pain and fear prevented it.

The incident resulted in a broken tailbone and knee cap. It kept me out of the saddle for more than two weeks. It is this incident that I will keep in the back of my head. This is the one I will replay over and over whenever something "goes wrong," whenever I think Jack is about to act out. No matter how hard I try to forget, the feeling of being thrown across the arena will never go away.

What started off as a nice, smooth process turned out to be more difficult than I ever could imagine. And while at the time that was where the fantasy I had dreamed up about retraining an ex-racehorse to be an amazing hunter/jumper ended, I did get back on, and I would continue to do so, because that is what you do as an equestrian. You dust yourself off, walk your horse back to the mounting block, and mount back up. It didn't mean it was easy, because it wasn't, but our story continues because I chose to keep riding.

SHATTERED DREAMS

The next few years went by just like a roller coaster, up then down, fast (and I mean that literally), slow and there were even a few hard stops along the way. This wasn't the horse I imagined, nor was it who I knew was in there. Something had to give, and considering all that they do for us, letting us ride them day in and day out and act almost as our therapist while we lay on them, rub on them, and treat them like children, it is a no-brainer that in return you should do what is best for them. And what was best for Jack? Well, that became clear. It was time to change barns.

The decision to change barns was scary, outside of our comfort zone, and not made lightly. I had been riding at Chasing Dreams Farms for fifteen years, and it had been Jack's home since he came off the track. But things just continued to not go well for us there. Between the constant bucking issues and me always ending up on the ground, those scary injuries, there were times when I found myself afraid even to get on him, for fear of what the outcome might be. I did my best and always put on a brave face, but it was hard sometimes. I never wanted to take him outside, and jumping anything higher than a little baby cross rail gave me massive anxiety. None of this was fair to either of us.

I knew that if I stayed, nothing was going to improve, but I also knew that there were no guarantees that things would change if I left. But what I did realize was that he needed a change of scenery. The two of us needed to take a different approach and get a fresh look into our partnership. That would be the only way we could move forward together and see what the next chapter might hold for us.

I contemplated leaving several times, even talking it over with my mom. "I know I could move him to other barns, but who would train him? Jayne has been with us since the beginning I don't even know where to start with someone new."

"I know but I don't like seeing you get hurt and unhappy. It might be time to really think about it." Our conversation always went the same, and yet we remained at Chasing Dreams.

I reached the point where I didn't have a choice. I really needed to consider our options. We felt trapped in our routine. I felt like everything I had dreamt up for Jack and I was slipping away. My dreams were being shattered. But when you are dedicated and patient, things have a way of working out. That was when my trainer was given the opportunity to begin a new chapter in her training career at another barn, and we jumped at the chance to move with her, with no expectations other than "Okay, Jack, let's give this a try." She has been the only trainer we have ever known; she knows what we do well, what we struggle with, how to get the best out us, and most importantly, she has a connection with Jack. We could not imagine having anyone else on our team.

"I know this isn't going to go over well, but I would really like to move Jack to the other barn. This is something we need; I want to give it a try."

"You and Jack will always have a spot with me, and if that is what you think is best, then absolutely, let's do it. I will take him when I move other horses."

Our last week at Chasing Dreams was very uncomfortable. Everyone looking at us like we were betraying the owners. They couldn't grasp the idea that this wasn't personal, that it was in the best interest of my horse. They all knew how things were for Jack and me, what we've gone through, so I thought we'd get more support. It didn't matter; we were leaving, and I was excited about our new adventure.

Jack is a Thoroughbred, a sport horse, and I am a jumper. We both deserved better, which leads us to where we are now—Jack and Lou and our new beginnings at Schuster Stables.

New Beginnings

Schuster Stables is very different from Chasing Dreams, in pretty much every way. The facility is set up as a show barn, which means everything is fancier. Our horses have access to grass turnout in huge pastures, and when the weather doesn't permit using those, there are several all-season paddocks. The horses never have to worry about being stuck inside. The facility also has two outdoor arenas and two indoor arenas, plus riding trails and a cross-country field. There is also a full-time staff, so our horses are always looked after.

It's Memorial holiday weekend, I am on vacation, so I can't be there with Jack when he's trailered to Schuster Stables. I make sure to have everything cleared out of my locker at Chasing Dreams before I leave, and I even receive text updates throughout the entire moving process. It is nice to be kept informed and that I can see that Jack made it safe and sound to his new home.

One of the things Jack is looking forward to the most is being able to be turned out with other horses. For some reason he was never allowed to have "friends" at the other barn. For horses socialization is very important, and this was one of our biggest complaints while we were at Chasing Dreams. Watching him interact with other horses is part of the experience.

We didn't move alone either. Several of us decided to switch barns, and we are all stabled together and share the same tack room.

I received video messages from my trainer after Jack's first official ride at our new barn and confirmation that he is responding nicely to his new surroundings. I am getting more optimistic each day and can't wait for our lesson when I return from vacation.

Our first ride once I got back is in the indoor arena, we decide to take things nice and slow. We didn't have the best rides before moving, and I am still a little apprehensive, being in a new environment. Jack, though, loves it. I could tell by the way he moves around the arena. With his ears nice and relaxed, he trotted around like he'd been living there his whole life.

We would have lessons for the next couple of

days in the smaller outdoor arena. Jayne being respectful of my lingering nervousness where outdoor riding is concerned. The lessons continued to go well, and we resumed jumping. Our first jumping lesson outside is a little sticky, but Jack remains unfazed, and it is finally time to move into the large show jumping ring.

"Let's finish up your lesson in the big arena." Jayne opens the gate, and we walk up the small hill to the show jumping arena. "Start trotting around on a long rein; keep him nice and relaxed."

After a couple of minutes getting acclimated to the larger ring and dusting off those lingering nerves, it was time to work—time to jump.

"Now stay trotting and take him over the blue flowers. If it goes well, keep going to your outside single and then your diagonal. One fence at a time."

It is at that moment with the way he carries me over those fences with no reaction to my imbalance or off distance to the fences that I know some big changes are in store for us, and I can't wait.

Making Strides

I blink and it has already been three months since I switched barns, although sometimes it still doesn't feel real. It is July in Northeast Ohio, and so far it has been a rather uncharacteristic summer, with excessive amounts of rain, no stretches of extreme heat or lengthy period of dryness. Jack has settled in nicely at Schuster's, and we have spent the last couple of months getting to know each other again and rebuilding that bond between horse and rider. Whereas before I dreaded having to go to the barn for fear of what might take place during our rides, now I yearn for it, cannot wait until it's time for a lesson, show, or just a day when I get to spend time with my boy.

I am up early Sunday morning so I can get to church before heading out to the barn. It's about a half hour drive to Schuster's, so I need to plan my day accordingly. My commute to my old barn was only about ten minutes from home, so the longer drive has taken some getting used to. It is mostly highway driving, so it seems to go by quickly. Sunday is the day Jack used to have off, but our routine has changed slightly. Now he gets Monday off, and I am at the barn on the weekends. So, my Sunday now looks like church, barn, errands (if I have any I chose not to get done during the week), and home, fitting in lunch and dinner somewhere between everything.

When I get to the barn it is around noon. There is never anyone around on Sundays, which is nice. I like when it is quiet and not a lot of hustle and bustle going on around us. Today is the day that I normally ride with our barn mate Hannah. We have a lot in common and have been friends for many years. Like me, she made the decision to move her OTTB Fender to Schuster's, which made my transition a lot easier. It is nice having good friends around.

"Good morning, Lou," I hear from around the corner of Jack's stall. Hannah has arrived. Lou is what everyone calls me. It is short for Louise, my middle name. "Ready to go for a ride?"

"Absolutely. It's finally a nice day, no rain. Fender is still outside in the front pasture. He and Jack were hanging out this morning, getting some fresh air and grass. You know how those two are together," I say with a snicker. Those two horses, while completely different in looks—Jack is a chestnut and Fender is a grey—they are mirror images of each other in personality. Both are goofy, super-affectionate, snack-loving giant Thoroughbreds.

Hannah brings Fender in from the pasture, and I take Jack out of his stall. I brought him in when I arrived a little earlier. I like to put him back in his stall for a few minutes after turnout to get some water, go to the bathroom, get a nice roll in, or whatever he needs to do before our daily ride.

We put our horses in crossties so they can get a nice grooming and tacked up for our ride. While not the most glamorous part of horse ownership, the time we spend grooming and visiting with our horses is just as important as the ride itself. The relationship with your horse starts from the ground and grows from there.

SETTING GOALS

While I am grooming Jack my mind wanders a little, just far enough to reminisce about when I said I would move him and some of what it entailed. Of course there was the obvious, leaving your so-called home, the fear of whether it was the right decision, but but there were also thoughts about what to do when you get there, and for me it is setting goals for myself. Goals would make the move seem a little less daunting. Truth be told they are for the most part things we could have accomplished at Chasing Dreams, but something was always getting in the way of us ever moving forward.

On my list are activities that many of my fellow barn mates have already mastered, but that didn't matter. They are for Jack and me and crossing them off one by one is our way of showing that we made the right decision and can in fact become the team

I know in my heart we are.

For instance, there are four major goals I want to achieve before the end of the summer season.

1. *Take Jack on a trail ride without our trainer— in a group or solo doesn't matter as long we won't have someone holding our hand.*

2. *Go out into the cross-country field and jump a fence, or even just get experience in the cross-country field in general.*

3. *Move up a division in hunters— the next one up is the 2'3" but I would settle with being officially in the 2' class. We've always done the 18" also.*

4. *Overcoming obstacles we may face, which could be anything: embracing our fear, personal obstacles, unexpected horse issues—anything. Just being able to push past and persevere.*

I look at the last one as an ongoing goal, something to continue building and working on throughout our journey.

When looking at those goals individually they seem insignificant, nothing earth shattering, but collectively they represent where I see things going with Jack and me. Goals are not something we would consider making in the past, certainly not ones that include trail rides and cross-country excursions, but now I find myself constantly looking to add more and more.

My mind returns to the present. The moment away leaves a smile on my face. I know the choice I made for my horse was the right one and that I will accomplish everything I set out to do this summer.

Jack is all brushed and ready for his saddle and bridle.

MENTAL STRENGTH

"Which arena do you want to ride in? They are all open. You okay with the big arena up top?" Hannah asks after we've finished tacking up our horses.

"Let's do it," I say, although the level of conviction in my voice is not that great. "I can't avoid getting back in there forever."

Hannah clearly saw my hesitation, the expression on my face a dead giveaway for what I am thinking. A few days earlier, during my lesson in the big outdoor jumping arena, the old Lou made her first appearance since our move, the Lou afraid of what might set her horse off bucking around the arena, the one where every time he perks his ears forward, she thinks this is it; he's going to take off, the one where no matter how hard she tries, she can't shake the nerves or sick feeling in the pit of her stomach. It was the first time since we arrived at Shuster's that we had an off lesson. We had been riding outside pretty much every day. I tried not to be to upset with myself over it.

But that is how it was at the old barn, on and off (with a lot of off days) for four years. Every ride I would wonder what the outcome would be. Would we finish our ride without me on the ground? Would I be brave enough to jump him? Would we make the canter work without racing off during the transition?

We loved our old barn; it was a wonderful facility owned by amazing people who taught me how to ride horses, for which I will be forever grateful. I made some lifelong friends in my time there, but something about the place did not bring out the best in Jack. We felt trapped in the arena, and I would get almost claustrophobic, tense up on the reins and pull on his mouth, all things that lead to potential disasters. It wasn't anyone's fault that we felt that way, and it wasn't all the time. Jack and I had some of our best rides to date at Chasing Dreams. But ultimately back then selling him sounded like the smart thing to do. Everyone thought so. We just weren't meshing as a jumping team, at least not on a consistent enough basis to be competitive, but I loved him, and we had a relationship, one I wasn't ready to give up on yet. Until

I was, when the rides stopped being fun, when going to see him felt more like a chore than a fun adventure. That was when I knew Jack needed to find someone better than me. "Okay, I thought, it's time to sell my horse."

My trainer knew it was the right decision long before I had come to terms with it, although she never pushed me on it. She waited until I was ready, until I finally realized that enough was enough, that loving my horse didn't mean I was right for him. So the sales ad went up and the potential buyers came in.

Months passed, and Jack was clear on who he was okay with riding him, telling prospective buyers right away "Nope I don't like you; this isn't going to work." I never knew a horse that was so opinionated in that way. It was like he knew what my plans were for him, and he was having none of it. Even though we weren't doing well together, he didn't want to leave. He wanted to stay with me. It was heartbreaking to think I would have to say goodbye to him one day; however, throughout the entire process I kept riding, because at that point we had nothing to lose. The rides became more fun, less stressful even. Fast forward, and here we are a year later, the same amateur owner and yet such a vastly different horse, a horse that is thriving and a rider that continues to improve with every lesson, including the "bad ones," which have gone from most rides to rare, and when they do occur, we can still find a way to get solid work done.

ADULT AMATEURS

"*A*re you showing next weekend?" Hannah asked.

"Um yeah, Hunters and Jumpers I think is what I signed up for this time." I reply while we are giving our horses a walk break and chatting. I still feel a little apprehensive about being in that arena, choosing to stay mostly to the half closest to the ingate where my brain thinks "This is safer." It isn't true. My horse does not care what half of the arena we are riding in, but that's the funny thing about being an equestrian; it is as much a mental sport as it is a physical one.

"Jayne really wants me to try the Jumpers also. I am just not sure I'm ready for that yet. I've only just started showing Fender, and he used to do Jumpers with Lana, so you know how he gets," she says with a smile and a neck rub for Fender. Lana is Hannah's daughter. Fender was her horse before she went off to college this past year, and Hannah officially took over as his rider. "What do you think?" she asks.

Hunters and Jumpers are vastly different equestrian disciplines. Hunters is all about the look. We all wear the same outfit: tan pants, black tall boots, and a dark-color show coat. We are judged based on how we look riding our horse; our body position, or *equitation,* as it is called; and on the way our horse looks going over fences. Jumpers, on the other hand, do not focus as much on the technical stuff. Your goal is to get over all the fences as quickly as possible without knocking any of them over. Hunters is the "pretty" discipline, and Jumpers is the "fun and flashy" discipline.

I like Hunters, I've been doing that style of showing for several years, although my equitation is not particularly good, and I cannot sit the trot to save my life. I am not the smallest rider, and I don't ride with the quietest of hands, so judges aren't drawn to me because of the way I look in the saddle. Jack, on the other hand, is flashy and catches your attention, which ultimately makes me look better.

Jumpers is something I've only recently started doing. My niece is getting more into that, and I want to be able to share that with her. Plus, with the Jumpers I tend to get out of my head more and allow Jack to ride the way he wants to and quite literally needs to be successful.

"You know, Hannah, I personally think Fender would be just fine in the Intro Jumper division. The fences are only two foot, which is what Jack and I do. Plus, you don't have to ride the course like a jumper, you can keep it more hunter-like, just get the experience. But I get it, if you don't feel like you're ready for that, don't push it. Things are going so well for you both. Build on that. Maybe add a two-foot Hunter class." I smirk. She knows my tone way too well by now. Our journeys have been so similar that like our horses, we are mirror images as riders.

"You're probably right, I'll think about it. Maybe we'll sign up and just see how Hunters goes and then decide."

OVERCOMING OBSTACLES

*I*t is about a half an hour later; we are just finishing up our rides when Jayne walks up. Jayne is our trainer, the one we moved barns to stick with. She is a little older than me. I am in my upper thirties, and she has been training both of us for the past several years, even before we bought our horses. In fact, Hannah and I both have our horses because of her. Jayne bought Fender off the track and restarted him. When he was ready, she sold him to Hannah and Lana.

Jayne is taller, slender, has dark hair, and used to be a competitive upper-level Eventer when she was younger. Her personal horse, Montana, who was her mount, is now leased out to a friend of ours looking to advance through the levels in the Dressage world.

"How was your ride?" Jayne asks us. She has a way of talking to Hannah and me that is different than she does her younger advanced riders, more "kid glove yet pushing" at the same time. I find it the perfect combination to get the best out of Jack and me.

"It was good," we reply, almost in sync.

"Wanna go on a trail ride? It should be dry enough for a short one."

"Hmmm." I reply and coyly look away. Since we moved, Jack has been doing exceptionally well. He has become less reactionary, and because of it has started learning the ropes of trail riding and has even ventured out into the cross-country field a couple of times. Both are on my summer goal list, and being able to start crossing them off so quickly has been quite an achievement. I was convinced that going out into the cross-country field was something I wouldn't get to do this year at all. Maybe not ever. It is nice to be proven wrong. We've gone on trail rides with our trainer, but she takes him alone after her rides. Never did I ever imagine that I would have a trail horse! It was one of my dreams when I bought him, and it looks like it may finally be coming true. "By ourselves?" My tone was oozing with sarcasm.

She laughed. "One day soon you both will be taking trail rides alone, I promise. But no worries; for now I'll walk with you."

The three of us leave the arena and head to the back of the property where the trails are. Schuster Stables is nestled on several acres of beautiful countryside. When the owner, JD Schuster, bought the barn about five years earlier, he made several improvements to the facility, including creating new trails for everyone to enjoy.

The trail ride was just as I hoped. It was nice and relaxing, even though I still get a little nervous that something is going to pop out of the bushes and startle Jack. But no, he never acts up. In fact part of me is quite sure he enjoys his long walks better than jumpers. We continued, my hands resting on the buckle of his reins, his head hanging nice and low, his ears flopping side to side, completely happy with life.

We finished our trail rides, untack our horses, gave them nice cool showers, and put them back outside for a bit while we cleaned their stalls. Sunday was the only day of the week that we needed to clean our own stall. The barn we are in has an amazing staff, and the horses get the best care. When people think of horses, they don't think about all the stuff that goes into taking care of them, and cleaning their home is just one small part of it. I don't mind it so much; I've been cleaning stalls on and off for years and have a pretty good technique by now. Dumping the wheelbarrow in one-hundred-degree heat, freezing cold, or pouring rain, on the other hand, is not much fun.

Overall today was a good day, and overcoming even the smallest of obstacles, such as getting back into the big arena, crosses another an item off our goal list. As an adult amateur equestrian, sometimes it is the smallest feat that will ultimately have the biggest impact.

DAILY CATCH-UP

On the way home I call my mom. This is our routine. We chat every day after I ride. Good or bad, she likes hearing all about it. "Hi honey, how was your ride?" she asks.

"It was good. I rode in the big arena with Hannah. Jack was perfect, of course, and I managed to keep my nerves in check."

"I told you everything would be okay after you were worried about how your last lesson turned out. Just breathe and keep going. Isn't that what I always say?"

"Yes, Mom, you always say that." She always tries to make me feel better by telling me it's okay to get nervous or that you know he isn't going to do anything. Oh, but my favorite is when she tells me, "What can he do to you that you haven't already been through? You've ridden through crazy racehorse and rodeo Jack." She isn't wrong. I've ridden him bucking across the arena, not the most pleasant experience at my age, but I can say that horse has turned me into the type of rider that I never thought possible because of some of those crazy shenanigans.

"Listen to me. I'm your mother."

"Yes, ma'am," I reply with a chuckle.

We chat for a few more minutes and hang up as I pull into my driveway. I'll spend the rest of the day cleaning up my house and taking my dog for a nice long walk. We don't get to do it as much as I'd like, since my new barn is farther away. Sometimes I feel like I spend more time at the barn these days than I do at home, which is another indication of how things have changed for us. Running to the barn to see Jack now means "I'll be there most of the day" instead of "I just want to get there and get home as soon as possible."

Tomorrow is Monday, and it's back to work, but unlike some people I do not mind going into the office. I work with a wonderful group of people, and my boss, who is also the owner of the company, does not mind when I need to take off early for horse shows and riding lessons or, well, anything horse-related, to be honest. It is nice to have that support, because riding is such a big part of my life.

It is also the beginning of show week.

On show weeks Jack doesn't normally get a day off. Between my trainer and me he gets worked every day to help get our head in the game, not like he needs it much. It is more to help keep him loose and in a rhythm before the show. Horse shows are always where Jack has been on his A-game. I never have to worry about that. He almost has a glow about him when he knows it is his turn to go into the arena, a "look at me" type attitude. I, on the other hand, am the one who needs extra encouragement on show days.

The work week goes on like any other, answering emails, filling out paperwork, taking phone calls, et cetera. When Wednesday comes along it's time for my lesson with Jack, our first since the slight breakdown we had the previous week and our first one before the show on Saturday. I try not to think about last week's lesson, but the bad stuff always seems to linger in my head longer than the good. "Not this time," I tell myself. "We've got this."

I leave work Wednesday around four o'clock. The barn is only ten minutes from my office, so it allows me plenty of time to get my stuff ready and Jack taken care of before our five o'clock lesson. Suddenly I remember that I didn't text my mom about letting my dog out for me today.

"Hey, Mom, I almost forget, but can you swing by and let my dog out for me?" I send via text message. I wait for the read receipt and little dots to appear, indicating she's sending me a reply.

"I was headed over there now. I remembered you asked if I could do it on Wednesdays for you," Mom replied.

"That's awesome. Thanks, Mom! I love you. I'll call you after my lesson." I always insert a smiley face emoji when I text my mom.

"Sounds good. I love you too, honey. Have a good ride."

LAST-MINUTE
ENCOURAGEMENT

*W*ow! What a lesson we had! I can hardly believe it was us out there. No fear, no butterflies, nothing. The moment we stepped into the ring I knew it was going to be good. I felt confident, ready. We started with a nice relaxing warmup, a little trot and canter work to get loosened up. Jack was very responsive to my aids, listening to everything I was telling him. When it was time to start jumping, he soared over every fence, making it look effortless. Each fence, the cute tacos and margaritas, the fun clouds, all of them, it was like the course was set up just for us, and we mastered it.

"If you ride like that on Friday and this weekend, no one will beat you. You looked amazing out there," Jayne said when we finished and were getting ready to make the walk back to the barn.

"Man, that felt good. After the other day I wasn't sure how today would be. You know how I have the tendency to dwell on bad lessons. And I am starting to think that he likes the jumps a little higher; that's for sure."

"Well, you also rode him the way he likes it today, which makes all the difference. You stayed out of his way, really engaged your core, and let him do his job. Plus I think you like the jumps a little bit higher also." A smile glances up at me from my trainer's face.

"I do. I really do!" I say, sounding a little more excited than a thirty-seven-year-old should, but heck, I love where things are headed with Jack and me.

The three of us are making our way down from the arena to the barn, partaking in a little chitchat about the plans for the rest of the week, when then there it was: the question I had been hoping she would ask me for as long as I've owned Jack, just never thought it would ever happen. It came almost out of nowhere. "So what are you thinking about WEC this winter? I know we talked about it briefly earlier this summer, but we're going to start making plans soon," my trainer asks.

A slightly shocked and confused look crosses my face. For a second all I wanted to do was scream, "HELL YEAH, WE WANT TO GO," but being a sophisticated adult, I think twice before responding. Plus, I don't think my brain is fully processing what is happening at this moment. "Oh, to be honest I haven't really given it much thought. I didn't think we would be in a good enough place even to consider being part of that trip." I'm lying. Of course I have thought about going to WEC, Wilmington Equestrian Center, one day. It is the fanciest venue in Ohio, and a lot of great horse and rider teams show there. But until recently, Jack and I were the background team. We were always there, and yes, we had shown some, but no one looked at us as a team headed anywhere.

"We should sit down soon and talk about it. In fact we should have a chat about how things are going in general. There have been a lot of positive changes with you this summer. We should explore that."

It is then that I realize we are part of the group, a real member of the team. I hadn't really felt that way at the other barn, not for a while, at least. I used to feel like we were the pity lesson, the lesson she was obligated to keep giving because I pay her, but she didn't really want to. There was a time when I even felt guilty that she still had to keep teaching us. It's not like we were learning anything;

it was more of a going through the motions type ride for Jack and me. She very easily could have just said she didn't see a reason to train us anymore, and I wouldn't have blamed her.

After moving to Schuster's and seeing Jack and I really come into our own, I was also starting to believe that we could be a successful team. Wow! That was a great feeling.

"Yeah, I think that sounds like a good idea also. There's totally been a lot of positive changes with us this summer," I said, "and I think continuing to set goals as we move forward is important for us."

Jayne and I are now back at the barn where Addison, the young woman who leases Montana, is getting settled into the indoor arena for her dressage lesson.

While I untack Jack, I make a mental list of what needs to be done for the show this weekend: clean bridle, clean saddle, pull mane, and give Jack a nice soapy bath. Show prep is a lot; there is so much to remember. Luckily this show is at our home barn, so I am less likely to forget something. Oh yeah, wash our show clothes. I still haven't done that laundry since the last show. I am certain they are still in a jumbled pile at the bottom of my garment bag.

When I finally get home, it is already after eight

o'clock, and so I don't forget again, I immediately grab my show clothes and put them in the washer. They aren't too bad. If I did manage to forget— again—they would be fine for the show. No one would even notice the stains on the pants. I mean it is a barn, after all, and anyone who works with horses does tend to get dirty.

After finally getting to dinner, hanging up the clothes, and feeding the dog, all my evening tasks are done. Tomorrow I have a meeting at work, and it is also the day I go back to my old barn for my niece's riding lesson. She is still part of that program since we are in the middle of a show season.

It's 10:45 p.m. My head hits the pillow.

SHOW PREP

*F*riday, 3:30 p.m., I finish up with all my work for the week, and I head out the door. Tonight we practice for the show. The arena will be set up with all the fancy jumps.

Jack and I normally pair up with Ellie, one of the junior advanced riders, and her horse Ruby for Friday night show prep. The arena can get a little crazy, a lot of horses and riders trying to get their time in and jump around. The younger riders aren't always the best at directions, and it isn't uncommon to get cut off when you're headed straight for a fence. It's all part of horse showing, but it can be a little frustrating at times.

This weekend Jayne has riders from both barns, Schuster's and Chasing Dreams, showing, including my niece, who will be doing Jumpers on Sunday. She rides in a higher division than I do, the Beginner Jumpers with fences that are two feet, six inches tall. It is nice because it gives me the opportunity to watch her.

The riders from Chasing Dreams are not scheduled to arrive until around six o'clock tonight, so we have plenty of time to get our practice in before that group gets into the ring. I take about twenty minutes to lunge Jack before our ride. Lunging helps him stretch and get nice and loose before he works. Ellie and I are in the arena warming up our horses and waiting for Jayne to arrive. There is another group of horses also practicing but they appear to be almost finished, so it looks like we'll have the ring to ourselves soon.

Jayne walks to the center of the ring. "Okay, guys, go ahead and pick up your trot and trot over the single brown diagonal fence."

Ellie and Ruby go first. Jack and I follow right behind.

"Now come up the outside line."

We both do a few more warm-up fences before starting on full course work.

"Ellie, I want you and Ruby to go diagonal, outside line, bending line, outside line." A bending line is jumping two fences in a row, but instead of their being in a straight line like the outside lines, they are set at a slight diagonal. "That was great. Just make sure you keep your leg on coming out of the turn, so she doesn't lose energy."

"Keep your leg on" is a horse trainers favorite saying and one I hear a lot when I am riding Jack.

"Okay, Lou, same course, but I want you to start at the canter this time. Really get him nice and forward before you head to your first fence."

The rhythm felt great, the ride felt great, and Jack felt great. But of course, no ride is perfect.

Same thing Jayne tells Ellie, "Don't lose the momentum in the corner. And really make sure you are looking ahead to your next fence and really engage your core. Don't forget to ride your flat work; you've been working hard on that part. Otherwise, it was a lovely ride." One area that Jack and I struggle with is our turns to the next fence. I've mentioned that I don't have the quietest hands when I ride, well that is part of the problem. I tend to pull on him with the reins instead of using my legs and seat. Pulling on him does nothing but make him fall out of rhythm and bulge to the opposite side of where I want him to go. We've been working on it a lot and we've improved tremendously over the past couple of months.

We ride for about another thirty minutes, going over different course options for tomorrow before the next group of riders makes its way into the ring. Hannah and Fender are in this group. While they are practicing, I can give Jack his bath and get his tack clean and ready for this weekend. Looking good is nearly as important as riding well when it comes to Hunters.

When I finish getting everything ready for tomorrow, I take Jack up to the show ring so he can munch on some grass, and I can check in with Jayne one last time before leaving for the night. It is only around 6:30, so I am making great time.

"Hey, Jayne, I am getting ready to leave soon, Jack is all good to go for tomorrow. I just wanted to double check what time you want me here in the morning and if you needed anything before I head out."

"Um, no, I think I'm good, thanks. How about normal time, eight o'clock?"

"Yeah, that sounds good. I'll see you tomorrow."

I walk Jack back to the barn and put him back into his stall. I give him his treats, scratch his neck, say bye to him, and head home.

"Eight a.m." That is what I tell my mom when she asks me what time we need to be there tomorrow. Even though I don't show until a little later in the day, Jayne likes us all to be there to support our fellow team members, plus it gives us the opportunity to school in the morning if we want. This is an important show for us. We are officially moving up to the Limit 2' Division, no eighteen-inches classes for this show, crossing off another item on my summer goal list. Depending on how things continue to progress, we may even get to try a round in the Suitable 2'3" Hunter Division before the end of the season.

"I want to leave by 7:30 at the latest."

"Okay, honey, I'll be at your house by 7:15. I love you." We hung up.

My mom is my rock, my support system. She is the one who got me into horses when I was a little girl; they were something she loved also. She has always been there, at every show, and up until I switched barns, she was even there for most of my lessons. She has seen me through my good moments, my bad ones, the smiles, and all the tears. She stayed with me when a bad fall sent me to the ER, drove hours in the middle of the night when my horse got rushed to the vet, and has been with me for everything in between. Just knowing that she is out there watching, cheering me on when I show, makes me less nervous. She always knows just what to say and, more importantly, what not to say.

SHOWTIME

*M*y mom and I arrive at the barn a little after eight. The show has just started. Our first riders aren't going for about another hour, leaving me plenty of time to get settled in and have a quick schooling session with Jack. I like having only a light practice or sometimes not doing one at all on show days. There is a thing with equestrians that we call "show anxiety," where you can be the best rider in the world but as soon as show day arrives and you step into the show ring and you know the judge is watching, you completely forget everything, what a posting diagonal is, what a canter lead is, and which fence you are supposed to jump next. Basically you forget how to ride. When I would hear people mention it, I thought it was more of an excuse for not riding well. I didn't know it was actually a thing, until I realized I have a textbook case of it, which is why I don't like to ride too much before showing. It keeps my nerves in check.

What a great morning for our beginner riders! They are showing in the lower ring and bring home some impressive ribbons, with one of our girls even winning the Champion Ribbon in the canter cross rails class. I always enjoy watching our other riders, especially the younger ones, and getting to be part of their journey from walk-trotters to horse owners themselves.

Following the conclusion of the academy classes in the lower ring, the show moves up to the big show jumping arena. This is where Hannah and Fender are getting ready to start their division, Hopeful Hunter 18".

"You got this." I say to Hannah. I give her a last-minute confidence check and go to stand next to our trainer to watch her round. Fender is an old pro at horse showing. He makes it look easy, and he takes good care of his rider. Their team has been fun to watch grow together these past couple of months.

"Wow! That was really awesome, you guys."

"Really? He didn't look like he was going too fast?" Hannah asks, winded from her ride. She always thinks he is going too fast, when honestly it usually looks like he's hardly moving. But like Jack, Fender is a big, powerful Thoroughbred, so even the slightest change in gait makes you think they are off to the races.

I chuckle a little bit before I respond. "OMG no. You looked great, and your outside line, by the judge, was pretty perfect. Hold on, let me go and get you some water."

"Thanks. Can we go over my next course?"

While we wait for Hannah's next round, we practice the course. It starts with the diagonal away from the ingate this time, then the outside line, bending line and ends with the outside judge's line. One thing I like about Hunter courses is that if you forget where you're going all you need to do is look down. Hunter courses have pretty little flower boxes set up on the side of the fence you are supposed to jump, which can be very helpful.

Her next two rounds are just as clean, and they walk away as the Reserve Champions of their division. Jack and I haven't won any of the big tri-color ribbons yet, but I have a feeling we are getting close. Winning ribbons is not what I set out to do when I show, but it has been a long time since we have won one, and doing so would show that our hard work is finally paying off.

There is a division between Hopeful Hunters and when Jack and I ride, so it is time to get ready and head to the warmup ring. One thing about horse showing is that sometimes it's a game of waiting around for hours doing nothing and then rushing to get to the ring. Luckily for us there are a lot of people in our class, fourteen, and we'll most likely go toward the end, allowing us the chance to take our time.

Okay, Jack is all tacked up, his mane and tail look great, and I spray him down with some show sheen for a little extra shine.

We're in the warmup ring, doing a little walk, trot, and canter work, getting all warmed up, even jumping a few fences when I hear Jayne say, "Ready to head up to the ring?"

"Yep, we're all warmed up," I reply.

As we walk up to the show ring, I give Jack some neck scratches—those are his favorite—and tell him it's time to go to work now.

"You're going to go after that bay over there. And remember, just ride every stride, keep him going forward, and look early during your turns. You got this." One last minute review of our course, and she escorts us into the ring.

We pick up our canter smoothly as we head to our first fence. It is the single brown diagonal with the purple flower boxes, the same one we practiced last night. We are jumping it toward the ingate. I can usually tell how the course will go based on that first fence. "Nailed it," I thought as we landed on the other side. Perfect strides, perfect distance, and rhythm. Six more fences to go, and each one rides just like that first fence. I exit the ring with a giant smile. I knew we rode great.

"That's a blue ribbon for Number 724, Whiskey Lullaby." I heard the announcer say over the loud-speaker. We did it! A blue ribbon! At that moment any lingering nervousness vanished.

"That was probably the best I've seen you ride him," Jayne says as we wait just outside the arena, learning our next course.

"You guys looked fabulous!" Hannah has fin-ished taking care of Fender and is now up at the ring to watch us ride.

"Keep riding the rest of your courses like that. There is nothing that I want you to change. Hannah, will you go over the next course with her?"

As we are going over the course, my mother walks over to congratulate us on our great ride. She brings me water and tells Jack how good a boy he is. She never misses the opportunity to praise us, even on days when I think I rode badly.

"Thanks, Mom. That did feel pretty great." A few more sips of water, and it's almost my turn to go again. My mother returns to her seat with the rest of our team cheering section.

The rest of our rounds are as good as I could have ridden them, I think. We missed a few distances here and there, but overall we rode cleanly. We didn't knock any rails down, and we hit all our strides. There was no funny business. I was super proud of our jumping today. But we aren't done yet. We have the dreaded flat classes next, the ones where they judge you not on fences but on how you maneuver your horse on the ground. This is where we struggle, and there are a lot of talented horse and rider combos in my division.

First up, under saddle. "Okay, Jack, we need to hit these canter leads, and we'll have a chance," I think aloud. We start the class going to the left, the direction where we struggle. Our trot work feels amazing; he is moving beautifully. Then I hear "Riders, canter your horses." I remember Jayne telling me not to rush the transition, to take a second and set Jack up properly. A little outside rein, inside leg, a smooch, and off he goes. I take a brief glance down. *The lead is good.*

"The lead is good, now let him go." I can hear my trainer from across the ring. She is the one person I can always hear when I am showing, no matter how loud the audience or the atmosphere gets.

I sit up in the saddle, loosen up on the reins

only slightly, and let Jack carry me around the arena. We change directions. The outcome is the same. "*Wow*" is all that I can think. We line up in the center of the arena and wait for the judge to place our class.

Finally, after what seems like an eternity, I hear the announcer say, "And now for the results of Limit Rider Under Saddle. In first place 653 Magic Mike, Second Place 724 Whiskey Lullaby . . ." The rest of the places are lost to me. Second place! No time to celebrate; we have one more flat class, equitation, the class where they judge how I look. We make our way back to the rail, tracking left, and wait for the announcer to start handing out our instructions. This ride isn't as clean, but I still think I did well.

"The results of Limit Rider Equitation. First Place 987 Daydream Believer, Second Place 105 Chocolate Martini, Third Place 653 Magic Mike, Fourth Place 724 Whiskey Lullaby."

TRI-COLOR
CONGRATULATIONS

*A*s we walk out of the arena to meet with everyone waiting to congratulate us, they start to announce the placings of the jumping rounds. I only listen for my name to be announced. "First trip over fences, second place 724 Whiskey Lullaby. Second trip over fences, first place 724 Whiskey Lullaby."

"Holy shit, Jack, you did it. We did it!" My excitement is almost contagious.

"Lou, you know what this means, right? You are going to win Champion," I heard Hannah say.

"No, I don't think so. That one rider placed higher than me in both the flat classes." One thing my trainer always gets on me about is that no matter how well I ride I always find something negative about it. Why can't I just accept that I might win? Why did I automatically remember that someone else placed higher than me in two classes? It's because up until recently I wasn't placing at all. Winning anything is a foreign concept for Jack and me.

"I don't know. I think Hannah might be right, but we'll have to wait and see. Regardless of the results, though, you rode amazing today." My trainer doesn't normally come out and say when she thinks you won or not, so her comment meant a lot to us.

It normally takes about a half hour or so for judges to tally the points and announce the division winners, so I take Jack back into the barn, untack him, and give him a nice cool shower. He worked hard for me today and deserved a little extra after-ride attention. After I get everything put away and Jack has been properly cared for, I head back out to the ring to watch the next set of our riders go.

"Honey you were amazing out there." I go and sit by my mother, and she gives me a huge hug. "Did you get your ribbons yet?"

"No, I was going to wait until they announced Champion, just in case. I am not sure if we have the chance, but our placings were really good."

"The Champion and Reserve Champion for the Limit Rider Division, your Champion is Number 724 Whiskey Lullaby, and your Reserve

Champion is Number 653 Magic Mike."

Just then I saw everyone rush over to congratu-late us. We were first out of fourteen riders. This is the moment Jack and I have been working so hard for, and it feels just like I thought it would.

"OMG, we did it! I finally won a tri-color rib-bon. I definitely need to take pictures this time," I say, laughing because they all know I am terrible at getting pictures taken at shows.

I go into the show office and gather my rib-bons and my prize for being Champion. When I come out Jayne is standing there waiting for me. "Congratulations. And not just for the ribbons but for getting out there and riding how I know you can. You should be proud of yourself. You've been working hard lately, and I think that this is just the start of your journey with Jack."

"Thank you. We couldn't have done it without you. Without you supporting us and pushing us and believing in us when I didn't always believe in us, I don't think we'd have made it here."

"I think it's safe to say that Jack isn't going any-where. Based on what I've seen lately, you and he are going to do some great things together. I am really happy to see it is all working out."

And just like that, not only are we winners but my horse is also officially no longer for sale. I didn't have to worry or think about it. He is staying, and he is mine.

I take my ribbons over to Jack so he can see our accomplishments, and with the help of my niece and Hannah and under the careful guidance of my mother, we get our picture taken with our Champion Ribbon, because no matter what happens tomorrow or in our rides to come, today that is what we are: champions.

ALWAYS A SETBACK

*I*t has been two weeks since we won our championship, and we are still reveling in it. Jack has been working hard since we moved barns, but especially on the weeks that we horse show. It isn't uncommon for horses to show signs of fatigue when they are in continuous work. Just like with people, even horses can feel overworked and need a break sometimes. Something about this time seems different though. It isn't like anything I have noticed in him before. He is extra difficult to get going, and while he has never been the most sure-footed horse, he has seemed to have a harder time lately, tripping a lot during our rides. To say I was concerned is an understatement.

I finally brought it up with Jayne. It has been about a week since I first noticed it, and she has a lot more experience with horses than I do. Maybe I am just overthinking things, trying to find something wrong, or maybe she has seen something also and might know what is going on. Either way, I needed to bring it up.

I didn't see her at the barn today when I rode. It is Saturday and I have been trying to go a little earlier in the day on the weekends. Contacting her isn't something I want to wait for, so I decided to give her a call. We are texters, so when one of us calls the other, we know right away that it is for something important.

"Hey, Jayne, sorry to bother you, but I knew I wouldn't see you today and I am a little worried about Jack."

"It's no bother, what is going on?"

"Have you noticed that he seems extra slow to get moving, even for Jack, and that he trips all the time? I don't know, something just seems off."

"I actually have noticed it; it wasn't as bad at first, but you are right, this past week something does seem off. I have the vet coming out to see Fender and Montana tomorrow and was planning on having her look at him while she was here. Is that okay?"

"Yes, absolutely. Thank you."

"No problem."

It is about two o'clock in the afternoon the next day when my phone rings. Jayne – Trainer appears across the screen. "Well this can't be good," I say to myself. If it isn't anything serious she just would have texted me "No worries, the vet said he's fine, just need to do a little A...B...C and he'll be back to normal."

This conversation is going to be different, an expensive one and a potentially season-ending one. I take a second to prepare for what she is about to tell me and answer the phone. "Hey, Jayne, did the vet look at Jack yet?"

"Yeah, she did, and unfortunately I don't have good news. She is worried about his tripping. I rode him when she was here, and it was pretty prominent. I also mentioned to her his unwillingness to go forward for you and his slight change in attitude."

"Okay, that sounds potentially bad. What does she think is wrong? What do I need to do for him?"

"She wants to test him for EPM. It takes about a week for the blood test to come back, and in the meantime she wants you to start him on meds."

Of course, I have no idea what EPM is but if it requires a blood test and immediate administration of meds, it can't be good. I turn to my trusted source, Google, to get some information.

EPM stands for equine protozoal myeloencephalitis and is a common neurological disease of horses in the Americas. Horses with EPM most commonly have abnormalities of gait but also may present with signs of brain disease. The disease ranges in severity from mild lameness to sudden recumbency and clinical signs usually are progressive.

Jack is showing many of the signs:

- *Frequent bucking*
- *Head tossing*
- *Excessively high head carriage*
- *Difficulty maintaining a specific lead or changing leads*
- *Difficulty negotiating turns*

I know what the official diagnosis is going to be just from reading up on it.

"Okay, I will get those ordered and start him on it right away. What does that mean for our training?"

"The vet wants him to stay out of work for two weeks just to make sure everything is headed in the right direction. After that he will go into light work, walk and trot only, with me for a week at which point we will do a reevaluation to determine whether he can resume work with you. I know this is not the news you wanted to hear."

"This is absolutely devasting. It happened so quickly, is this something I should have noticed sooner? I read that it can be deadly and horses can become dangerous to ride."

"She thinks we noticed it soon enough and that he should respond well to the treatment. It isn't curable, so you might have to treat him in the future, but he should return to normal. And no, you didn't miss anything. This is something he could have had for years, and it is just now showing up. You did the right thing by telling me you were concerned, so let's get him better. The rest will work itself out."

There it was: our first major setback since our newfound partnership. In fact I have been pretty lucky with Jack health-wise. Apart from his few nights' stay at the emergency vet to treat ulcers when I first got him, he didn't really need to see the vet. I hope that after his three-month treatment of anticoccidial drugs that our vet said is the standard treatment period for EPM, he should be just fine.

The next two weeks were rather uneventful. I would go to the barn, hand walk Jack for a little bit because he wasn't allowed to have turnout until his follow-up bloodwork was done, give him his meds, and basically just wait until it was time to get back into the saddle.

The day I brought Jack to his new home –
February 3, 2019

Jack's very 1st horse show, ridden by our trainer – CVF March 2, 2019

Jack and Alexis' very first show together – Walk/Trot division – CVF April 7, 2019

The first ribbons Jack and Alexis earned together –
Walk/Trot division – CVF April 7, 2019

First time showing in Walk/Trot/Canter division – CVF
May 5, 2019

The first-time trying jumpers – Crossrail Division –
December 5, 2019

Learning the ropes of outdoor riding our first summer
together. We would spend a lot of time on crossrails –
July 2019

Our first trip to Hinckley Equestrian Center. Jack and I moved up to the Hopeful Hunter 18" Division on this show – July 18, 2020

After over 2 years of ownership Jack and I finally moved up to the Limit Rider 2' Division – May 15, 2021

We had the opportunity to try our hand at dressage and stadium jumping under the lights; my mom as always was right there to support me – HEC September 11, 2021

*Combined Tests have become a favorite for Jack and me.
This one at a primarily open space facility which was a
major step for us – BPC March 25, 2022*

A little barn fun show for Halloween with "Jack and Coke" – October 22, 2022

Major changes for Jack and me this year. After 4 years Jack moved to a new home – May 2023

Jack and I's first time in the Cross Country field –
June 24, 2023

We've been getting more interested in jumpers as we've grown as a team – HEC Jumpers August 27, 2023

No matter what the outcome of the ride is, good, bad, or anywhere in between, it is important to always leave the ring with a smile on your face!

Your horse works hard for you, day in and day out. Always remember to thank them, give them praise, love, neck scratches and treats! They've earned it.

After 5 years of ups and downs, Jack and I have finally moved away from crossrails. While we don't jump these big fences on a consistent basis, we can jump them and will continue to work every day to make them our norm —
August 2, 2023

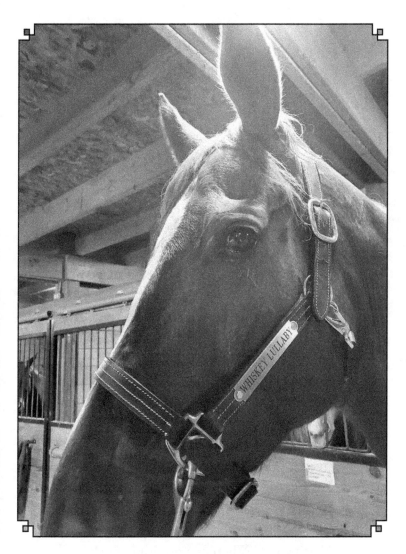

Jack, my "Whiskey Lullaby"

THE NEXT STEP

*T*wo weeks of no riding and no turnout for Jack felt like an eternity. Being able only to hand walk him around, with no riding, is starting to drive both of us crazy. A Thoroughbred without turnout is like a ticking time bomb. They really need exercise to reduce stress and get their energy out, and I think Jack is over his stall rest and as ready to get back to work as I am.

I am walking Jack around the arena while Hannah is riding. She says, "I had to go through that with Fender when he hurt his leg. It's not fun, but Jack will be fine. When does he get to go back to work?"

"Jayne is going to start riding him again tomorrow. I am going to come and watch; I want to see how he looks." I gave him his typical scratches on the neck.

"That's good. When do you think you'll be able to start riding again?"

"Hopefully next week, as long as he hasn't turned into a fire-breathing dragon." We both laughed, and I gave Jack a playful glance.

The first ride after having those weeks off was rough, according to my trainer. He was "feeling his oats," so to speak. She took that week to get his attitude right before I was allowed back on. With horses you never know what might happen, so it's important to have a solid team around you.

According to the vet we have done everything right, and Jack looks good back under saddle. His follow-up bloodwork is already showing signs of improvement even after just two weeks of meds. I was feeling good about things.

I get the go ahead from Jayne to start lessons back again, although we aren't going to be doing any jumping right away, which is okay with me. I want to work on my flat work anyway, and I have also been talking with her about potentially learning more dressage with him. And even though we haven't jumped in a couple of weeks I feel like our jumping is finally in a place of consistency, so the timing seems right to start including additional areas of riding to our repertoire. We have already been doing some intro and first-level movements as part of our flat work exercises, but I want to take what we have been learning and advance.

Hannah and Addison are sitting in the viewing area of the indoor arena while Jayne is giving Ellie a lesson. We were lucky to have a couple of weeks without rain, so at least during Jack's hand-walking time we were able to do it outside. That pleasure didn't last long, though. The past few days it has been raining steadily which meant no riding outside.

"So I hear that you guys are back to work and you're looking to start doing more dressage," Addison comments. She is always willing to give advice whenever one of us expresses interest in dressage. She and Montana have become quite the team this past season, so we heed her words.

"Yeah, I have even started looking at saddles. Jayne told me what size to be looking for, and I know I won't be buying a new one just yet, but you can find some nice used ones."

"I like this brand of saddle. It's what Jayne's and mine are. Let me send you the Facebook link for the resale site. Ellie just got hers from there."

"That would be great. Thanks."

Finding the right saddle was not an easy task. I looked at several online and tried three different ones before finally settling on one. It isn't the fanciest or newest, but it is comfortable, looks nice on Jack, and most importantly fits both of us well.

"Now that you've got your saddle and there are no restrictions on Jack, we should talk about your lesson and show schedule for the rest of the year."

"Sure. What were you thinking?" Jayne and I are sitting in the kitchen area at our barn.

"Well, I still think you should consider going to WEC with us in December, but you still have time to decide. You know we are putting on the combined test at the end of September. You should enter with Jack. This will be the first time you'd get to show in your dressage saddle, so it'll be good practice. We should also start incorporating more dressage lessons into your routine from now on."

The summer has flown by, August is over, and it is hard to believe we are already talking about shows at the end of September and even into December. I was already thinking about doing the combined test. I have competed in them in the past and really enjoy how they are set up. Combined tests consist of two out of the three event disciplines, usually dressage and stadium jumping.

"I know for sure I want to do the combined test. I like those. And I would really like to go to WEC. It's just . . . it's a lot of money, and I know we won't win anything, but I want to at least know that we'd put good rounds together."

"That's great. We will get you signed up for the CT and start working on your dressage tests, I think Starter level will be good for you guys."

I had a sense that she was a little disappointed that I wasn't quite ready to commit to going to WEC with the team yet. It's a big decision for us. The venue is massive, there are a lot of things that Jack hasn't seen before, and come on, up until a few weeks ago he was still technically for sale. I am still trying to catch up to the fact that I am keeping him.

"You two have had quite the summer so far. Did you ever think it was going to be like this when you decided to move him here?" she asks.

We don't often talk like this. I mean we are friends, but our conversations are not usually on the "let's have a nice chat" side. They are normally more "trainer to rider." It is kind of nice.

"To be completely honest, no, I didn't. I knew he would be different. Ever since the first time we brought him here for a show, we always enjoyed this place, but to this extent, no. The horse that I have now is not the same horse that left Chasing Dreams back in May."

"It's clear that you made the right decision. I

know it wasn't easy, but you should be proud of what you've done so far. I mean you rocked it at the last show."

I smile, shake my head, and reply with a simple "Thank you. I am proud."

THE SPIRAL

*W*e are well into September and the combined test is coming up quickly. Jack and I have been working hard on our dressage movements, and we even resumed our jumping lessons. Jayne has started putting the jumps up a little higher also. We even managed to cross the last remaining item off our summer goal list: we did a trail ride with Hannah, just our horses and us, no trainer there to hold our hands. Was it scary? Heck yeah, it was. All I kept thinking was some silly deer or cute little bunny rabbit was going to come darting out of the bushes and that would be it. But of course none of that happened. Hannah and I kept talking the whole time, and all Jack cared about was trying to sneak some grass or an apple off the bushes as we passed by.

The good days far outweigh the bad days since our move to Schuster's, but that doesn't mean there aren't any bad ones. It is hard to describe what causes me to "spiral," what makes me forget Jack isn't the same horse he was at the beginning of the year, that insignificant things don't bother him anymore, and that I know how to ride him. But it still happens. The difference is that when it does hit, I have found a way not to let it consume me. That gut-wrenching feeling is just that, a feeling, not a ride-ending worry anymore.

My lesson starts off like any other, warming up at the walk and then the trot. Nothing seems out of the ordinary. In fact Jack feels great. After starting his EPM treatments he has been more willing to go forward, and there hasn't been nearly as much tripping, so I am hopeful this setback is finally behind us. I also think all the dressage work that we have been doing has been good for him. It helps loosen him up and stretch his neck down nicely.

But that's where things change. I can't tell you why, but suddenly I am afraid. *Fear*, that damn four-letter word that has plagued Jack and me for years, is back again. Is it because he perked his ears at something? Is it because he got a little "fast" during our trot work? Did I suddenly just remember that he wasn't ridden for a couple of weeks? I wish I could tell you. All I know is that it is there, and my trainer could see it plain as the day on my face.

"What's wrong? Every part of your body right now is telling him something is wrong. You have a death grip on the reins, and you're collapsed over his neck. I need you to breathe. Take a walk break and breathe." Jayne is being super supportive, but I can tell she gets annoyed and frustrated with me when I get like this. I don't want to be like this, but sometimes I can't help it. Our history makes it hard to trust him 100 percent all the time.

I can feel Stacey, the other trainer at our barn, stare at me as I walk past her. She is also teaching a lesson in the big outdoor arena today. It is as if she is saying "Get a grip" or something. Truth be told she probably doesn't even notice what is happening with me, and even if she did, she doesn't care. She is too busy teaching. One thing that I've noticed with Jack, and it carried over from our old barn, is that we tend to tense up when other people are in the arena with us, especially when they are taking lessons. We've been working on it, and it has gotten much better, but we still have work to do for sure.

"I don't understand why you do this," Jayne continued, her tone slightly angrier than before. I can hear the irritation in her voice. "He has done absolutely nothing wrong for you to be pulling on him like that. You need to trust him."

"I don't know what caused it. I can literally feel it. I've never actually noticed it before, but this time I can see myself grasping the reins." That is the truth. When she would tell me what I was doing to him in the past, I didn't understand. I was too afraid to really care. I just wanted to be done and off as soon as possible. But this time is different. I don't want to be like this. I want to get through it, to understand what I need to do, and most importantly I know that with the way Jack has been behaviorally lately, I know I can.

"It's okay. He's being super. He's not reacting to your nerves and anxiety, so let's do this." Jayne continues with a set of instructions on how to get me to relax and still have a productive ride.

For the next twenty minutes we work on our flat work. Trot, canter, trot, canter, change direction, trot, canter, trot, canter. "This is all about getting your confidence back. That's it, bring his head down, now make the circle bigger. Perfect. Change direction across the diagonal and do it on the far end of the arena."

Slowly I relax and the fear begins to be less and less. It is still there, but it isn't taking over anymore. No matter what, I will not let it consume me ever again.

"Good, now stay trotting and go over the blue diamond fence."

We make our way to the fence. I can feel my anxiety building slightly.

"That's it. Now go into your two point and put your hands on his neck. Let him do the work for you. You do nothing up there."

We jump.

"Perfect, now do it again. Stay on a circle and just keeping doing that same jump a few more times."

It is like magic. Once we focus on something other than what *might* happen, we are able to have a productive lesson. We work around a single fence and then finish off with two full courses. Are they perfect? No. Will they win any gold medals? Definitely not. But that isn't the point. The point is to show us that even when I am starting to spiral back to my old self, even when that little fear monster shows up, we can still be successful.

"I understand why it is hard for you sometimes. He put you through hell in the past. But that was then, and he is different now. I really need you to trust in your riding and trust in Jack. I wouldn't make you keep riding if I thought for one second he was going to do something bad."

A look of disappointment is now on my face. I know I can do better, and I need to do better.

"Don't dwell on it, you've never given up before, and you still had a great lesson. You jumped everything I asked and finished on a really nice course. Friday will be even better, and you won't even remember what made you nervous today."

I feel reassured as we walk back to the barn.

GIRLS NIGHT OUT

a group of us "barn moms," as I like to call us, have been getting together about every other month for the last several years. Their girls and my niece have all been teammates for many years, and even after some of us left to move to a new barn we still maintained our friendships.

It has been a while since the last time we were able to all get together. We have been talking about it since I moved barns back in May, but there hasn't been a time that works well for all of us.

Finally we find a night that is convenient for everyone, an evening when we can all get together for dinner and drinks, just a chance for all of us women to hang out away from the barn and spend a little time together. Our routines are all pretty mundane: work, barn, home, repeat.

We pick a place centrally located for everyone. With each of us living in different cities it isn't easy, but for the most part no one has too far a drive. Nothing fancy, just a nice casual restaurant with an outdoor patio; the weather is rather warm for the middle of September in Ohio, so we thought sitting outside would be nice. It is a Thursday night, it's not busy and we have no problem getting a table to seat all of us. I order my usual, Jack and Coke, my favorite drink and how my horse got his name.

I took the opportunity to make the first toast. "I would just like to say that I really enjoy these dinners. Having this time with all of you and having all the support you give Jack and me makes a world of difference, so thank you."

This is the first time that Jayne came to one of our dinners. In the past she was always teaching lessons, so she is a welcome addition to our party. Hannah raises her wine glass and takes the opportunity to make a toast in Jayne's honor. "Here's to Jayne for letting us tag along when she moved, our horses for taking it all in stride and taking care of us, and of course to us. We are a special group and the way we encourage each other has been amazing. Thank you."

Glasses clink across the table and we each participate in various rounds of small talk while we wait for our food.

"So, Lou, have you thought any more about going to WEC with us?" asked Lisa, Ellie's mom.

I take a sip of my drink before answering. I don't want to give anyone the impression that I have decided one way or the other yet. "Oh, for sure I've been thinking about it, especially after we won our championship, but then Jack got sick, so I kind of put it on the back burner. I would love to be part of it. I just want to make sure that we are definitely ready for it all."

"Where were you leaning before Jack got sick, and where are you leaning now?" chimes Katie. Katie is one of the moms from Chasing Dreams. She and I are really close friends. Her daughter and my niece have been riding together for almost ten years now. She was very supportive of my move to Schuster's.

"Before? Before I would say I was definitely leaning more toward yes. But now, now I am not so sure we're ready. We lost a couple of solid weeks of training time. I mean, I am totally scared shitless about it. All I think about are the giant screens and massive arenas. But Jayne has been super supportive of us going, so right now I would like to think we're going to go. *But* . . . I have not made any official decision yet. You said I had until the end of October before I had to say for sure, right?" I look over at Jayne for affirmation.

"Yep, that's right. I need to start getting the paperwork together the beginning of November, and you'll need to get Jack registered and microchipped if you decide to go."

Lisa took Ellie last year for the first time and they are planning to go again this year and said, "It is a lot of fun; we get a house right by the venue for the week and rent a golf cart. The girls spend most of their time at the barn and we are the errand runners, but it is wonderful experience."

We continue chatting about horses, of course, and our personal lives and work, and like any other group of women, we gossip a little also. It is exactly what we needed. Sometimes riding horses, or just life in general can be stressful, but having these women in my corner makes all the difference. Does that mean we always get along? Absolutely not. I get jealous sometimes when their daughters place better than me at shows or when Hannah's horse gets complimented but Jack doesn't. But do we always support each other? Yes, absolutely, because we've shared the same experiences. We've been through successes, failures, disappointments, and achievements. We genuinely care about each other.

The Decision

*I*t's the next day, and after work I call my mom on my way home. I need to discuss whether I am going to WEC with the team, and it is her opinion that I value the most.

"Well, honey, you know what I am going to say. You should go. What reason do you have for not going?"

My mom is always telling me I can do anything where Jack is concerned. Even at our lowest points she would still say, "Oh Lou, just get out there and ride. It'll be fine." Usually she is right, but sometimes I must remind her that it isn't always that simple.

"I guess I am just still a little nervous about things. Okay, it's true he's had a great summer, but he hasn't traveled anywhere for a show in about a year, and for our first off-site one to be at WEC is a little intimidating for me. There are a lot of things that can go wrong. Plus, you know me. I don't want to make a fool of myself out there, especially against the other girls."

"I understand your worries, but you don't know for sure any of that is going to happen, and you won't know unless you go. So what if you go out there and have bad rides? You still went out there and tried. And Jack will get some rated show experience that you keep talking about and you'll get to see what it's like riding in those fancy arenas. Plus I wouldn't mind watching you show in one of those fancy arenas either."

I can hear her smiling from the other end of the phone as she says that.

She is right. They all are. We should just go. I really want to, and honestly, we have nothing to lose. Well, okay, that isn't entirely true. We have a couple thousand dollars to lose, but the experience we would gain and the time we would have down there would be worth it.

In true Lou fashion I spent the next couple of days going back and forth weighing all the pros and cons and should I and shouldn't I's. I felt like I was trying to talk myself out of it almost as much as I was trying to convince myself I was good enough to go with them.

My mom is always on team "you can do anything Lou." For this decision I need to get some advice from individuals whose viewpoints are a little less biased, which is where my best friend trio of Joc, Maria, and LJ come in. You couldn't ask for a better group of friends, and when I ask for advice they never hold back.

We meet up at Joc's the following Monday night for drinks. We all work in such different industries that Monday seems to be the only day that works well for all of us. Her house is our typical meeting place, and she makes the best margaritas.

"Okay, ladies, I need your opinions on something. *Honest opinion,*" I remind them, so they don't tell me what they think I want to hear.

After the brief synopsis of my WEC dilemma and my laundry list of reasons why I should or shouldn't go, I pause for a moment and wait to hear their thoughts.

"Lou, I have known you since we were ten years old. Horses have always been your life, and doing a show like this has been your dream. *Girl, go!*" Maria is my oldest and dearest friend. She always cut to the chase.

Joc and LJ share similar responses. "I agree. I've never seen you show, but I know how much you love it, and if you can afford it, then go. Plus it's not like you invited yourself; your trainer literally asked you about it. I would say that's a clear indication of how she feels."

I wasn't sure what I was expecting them to say, but I knew it wasn't a resounding *go* from all of them, especially Joc, who usually errs on the side of caution with most things in life.

They are right, I am being completely ridiculous. If they didn't want me to go, they wouldn't have asked me in the first place, and with that, the decision was made, and it was time to make it official. I still have a month to think about it before I have to say for sure, but there is no reason for me to delay any longer. I knew I was going. Time to tell my trainer and start the paperwork.

THE PAPERWORK

I pick up my phone, open my text message with Jayne, and start typing. It is early Tuesday afternoon, so I know she isn't teaching a lesson right now.

"Hey, Jayne, you probably already know what I am going to say, but I've thought about this and debated it, and I would like to go with you to WEC if you still have a spot for me. We can talk about it later at my niece's lesson or tomorrow when I ride, but I just wanted to tell you my decision." I include a smiley face at the end of the message, hit Send, close the phone, and wait for the reply.

It's been a few hours and still no reply. Hmm, that isn't like her. Of course my mind went straight to "Maybe something changed and there isn't a spot for me anymore." I decide not to dwell on it, I will be seeing her this evening. We can talk about it then. I pulled into the driveway at Chasing Dreams. It is still a little weird going back there, and I go only once a week now to watch my niece's lesson. Jayne is already here, so there should be time for a quick chat before she starts teaching. I wasn't going to approach her though; I didn't want her to know I was slightly agonizing over it.

This barn is so different from Schuster's, it is hard to believe that this is where I spent half my riding career. I spend a few moments recollecting past events before my niece comes by for a quick hello and a hug. If my mom is my biggest supporter, my niece knows I am hers. I would do anything for that young lady, and one day Jack would be her horse. She has an incredible talent, and this past year she has come into her own as a rider.

I make my way over to the viewing area of the indoor arena where my mom is already seated. Unlike at my barn, when it rains here, people can't ride outside until the ground dries out, which can take anywhere from a few days to a week, depending on the weather.

Jayne sees me and walks over. She has a rather large packet of papers in her hand. "I got your text."

I can see a small smile on her face.

"And what do you think? Is that okay? I would really like to go."

"One hundred percent yes. I put this together for you a while ago. I have just been waiting for you to decide until I gave it to you." She hands me the packet. "This is everything you need to know about going to WEC. What vaccines Jack needs, what he is or isn't allowed to be on, where we are staying, stabling, entry fees, pretty much everything. I even updated the cost breakdown for this year and added a timeline, so everyone knows when things need to be done by."

"Wow, this is a lot." When she hands me the packet, I flip through it really quickly. It looks more like an Anne Rand novel than a show packet.

"Yeah, it isn't like going down the street to a show, these A-rated shows are pretty extensive. It'll be worth it, though. I don't want to put any entries in for you until the last minute, though. I am not sure what fence height we should put you in yet. You are kind of between levels, so let's see where things end up."

"Sounds good to me."

Jayne heads to the center of the arena to start the lesson. I sit with my mom, who brings my niece to all her lessons, and we look over the packet.

"I guess it's real now, isn't it, Lou?"

"Yep, Mom, no turning back now."

I set the packet on the table and turn to watch my niece's lesson. Our journey to WEC has officially begun.

SMALL IMPROVEMENTS

*J*ust like that, September ends.

The combined test that our barn put on is a tremendous success with competitors coming from all over the area to get a chance to try something new and check out the cross-country course.

We spent the last two weeks leading up to it working mostly on our dressage, our jumping now feeling solid. We compete in the starter division, which includes a walk, trot, canter dressage test and a two-foot stadium jumping course. It is usually a larger class since a lot of riders who are just learning dressage tend to enter it. Dressage is all about the connection you have with your horse and how seamlessly the horse transitions from one movement to another. Everything should look like it flows together with no choppiness. The horse's head shouldn't be flailing around in the sky. Some people refer to it as "horse dancing," which is a pretty accurate representation of what it looks like. Personally I think it is harder than jumping, and when you've mastered a movement, it is beautiful and rewarding.

One thing that is important for me to remember during our dressage test is that you aren't allowed to talk. I use a lot of verbal commands when I am riding Jack, but unfortunately they are not allowed during your dressage test, and you will get marked down for it.

"Remember, no talking," is the last thing I hear Jayne say before I start my warmup and wait for the bell to sound. It is our turn to go.

Jack and I did well in our combined test. I knew what areas I would score higher or lower in, based on the feedback I had been getting from Jayne in our lessons. Jack and I received higher marks on the movements going to the right. We scored down on our canter transition to the left and on our free walk because it is, for lack of a better word, not so free. We had an amazing trot to halt down center line and came away with nice scores on those.

After we finish our class, I head over to the show office to collect our score sheet. Another reason I enjoy dressage so much is that they let you take home your score sheet, which provides a lot of valuable feedback on what you did well and what you need to work on. Both the jumping disciplines, hunters and jumpers, do not do it, which makes it difficult to see what areas you need to focus on to improve.

"Did you go get your score sheet?" I ask Hannah. We did the same division. She and Fender placed a little better than I did, fourth, compared to my sixth, but I didn't care; we were eliminated from the last two combined tests we entered because we didn't get through the entire jump course.

"Yeah, we did good for our first dressage test. How about you?"

"Jack and I improved on a few things, especially on our canter circles. We didn't score great on it, but we hit the left lead canter this time. I was so proud of him." I laughed. "This comment has been on all my score sheets." I point to the section on my test where it says, *Lovely horse, need to work on maintaining connection.* "We'll figure it out eventually."

TRAVEL JITTERS

*a*fter the combined test at the end of September was finished, I decided to forgo the next show being held at Schuster's. Instead taking the opportunity to help as part of the show crew, watch my fellow riders, and just get to enjoy a show without the stress of participating. Jack and I have done quite a bit of showing lately, and I felt like we deserved a little break.

There is one last outdoor show of the season remaining, and it is being held at another facility close the us. We have shown there many times in the past, and it is the same facility where Jack had his very first horse show, but it has been about a year since we've been there. I feel like it is the perfect opportunity to trailer him off property and see how things go.

"I have you and Jack, Ellie and Ruby, and Liz and Donatello as all going to Harmony Acres next weekend. Is that right?"

"Yes, we are going." I answer.

"We are going too," I hear Liz and Ellie respond.

"Perfect. We will plan on getting there Friday afternoon. I will be bringing the other barn also, so if you can get there early to school, that would be great."

Since the show is off property, I need to make sure I pack everything in our tack trunk that I will need for the weekend. It has been a while since I've gone through it, so it probably needs a good cleaning out and restocking of items.

"I am really nervous about taking Jack. It has been so long since he went anywhere or we've shown anywhere different," I tell Hannah during our typical Sunday morning ride.

"I can understand that, but try not to be. Use this as the chance to dust off the cobwebs and get yourselves ready for WEC. This will probably be your last opportunity to take him somewhere."

"That is my plan. Plus I need to see just how well we are actually doing together, and this is a huge test for us. What is it we always tell each other? One ride at a time."

"One ride at a time."

Typical show week: work, two riding lessons, and getting everything packed up before we head out. Jack worked well this week, even on the days my trainer had him, which was a good sign, I thought.

I arrive at Harmony Acres around four o'clock Friday afternoon, find our stalls, and start getting Jack ready for schooling. He seems nice and calm, with no pacing around in his stall or signs of anxiety.

"He got here just fine, no problems loading him on or off the trailer."

"Thanks, Jayne, I've been thinking about it all day."

"Go ahead, get him tacked up, I'll lunge him for you, and then we can go outside and practice a little bit."

I hand Jack off to Jayne so she can get him lunged for me and ready to ride. I mention maybe having her hop on him first if he seems like he might be a little anxious. Even with all the issues the two of us have had at shows or in lessons, I am always the one to ride through it. Asking my trainer to ride my horse before I get on is not something I like to do unless absolutely necessary. It says a lot about us adult amateur riders that we can get through the rough moments ourselves.

"Alright, here you go, he's perfect. You can go ahead, take him to the outdoor ring, and get on.

Just start walking around nice and relaxed and get yourself comfortable out there."

Luckily the show didn't seem as big as some of the ones we participated in this summer. Kids were back in school, and the college teams all started their seasons. It is mostly the local barns this time, which makes me feel better. I knew we wouldn't have a crowded arena to ride and show in.

"See? I told you it would be just fine. You guys did great out there."

"Thanks, I was definitely nervous, but after we trotted around a little bit and especially after that first jump I felt much better. I think it's going to be fine tomorrow. I don't think I am going to do any schooling in the morning, though."

"That sounds like a good plan. Give him a nice lunging session when you get here, and he should be good to go after that." Jayne finishes up with me and is getting ready to start working with the riders from Chasing Dreams.

I use the good ride we had to my advantage. Feeling confident, I take Jack for a walk around the property to cool down.

He performs just like I need him to on Saturday. I decided to add in a warmup round, which I don't normally do, but anyone could see I was a little nervous when I initially got on. Jack didn't react to anything I was doing, which allowed me to relax, get through it, and turn in a decent round.

I am grateful that my mom, who basically never misses a show, and my niece are here to cheer us on. Since it is an off-property event, I especially wanted my support team there, reminding me I did good out there, and saying, "He looked great." For some reason the more they say it the easier it is for me to believe it.

"Congratulations, Auntie. You and Jack looked really good out there." My niece waits for us at the ingate after our round. She walks with us into the warmup ring and gives Jack scratches on the neck.

"Thank you. I think this is a good test for us, and so far it seems to be going well."

The Harmony Acres show was exactly what I needed. We dusted off our travel jitters and got some much-needed experience at a different facility. It was like riding a bike; Jack knew just what to do and rode like a champ. I couldn't have asked for a better ending to our outdoor season.

Season Wrap Up

With the completion of the Harmony Acres October Schooling Show, our summer show season is officially over. We have done a lot of shows this summer, with a few of them even being back-to-back. I feel like we gained a lot of experience this season, and even though we didn't take home any end-of-the-season Championship awards, we did at least place for the first time, seventh place for the season. What an accomplishment! In a matter of months we went from "I am afraid to ride my horse" to "my horse is amazing, we win things together, and now we are planning a trip to WEC." Quite the turn of events, for sure.

The next show season we will be moving indoors, since we live in Ohio and there aren't many opportunities to ride outside past October. I chose not to enter Jack into any of the November or December schooling shows. We both deserve a break from showing, and since I had decided to attend WEC this year, I need to save the money.

We use the rest of our outdoor lesson time to work on fine-tuning our riding a little bit. We know that the weather is going to push us all inside soon, so we want to take advantage of it while we still can. Jayne has us working on keeping a balanced rhythm throughout the entire course and working on pushing him forward to lose strides and holding him back to add them. She's also making the courses more difficult, incorporating higher fences and oxer-type jumps.

"All these things we have been working on will be important when you see how the courses are set up at WEC. Even though the height of the fences is the same, the fillers and size of the arena make them look much bigger."

"That makes sense. Even at some of the places we show around here, the fences can actually look different heights."

"The most important thing for you to remember is to maintain a consistent rhythm throughout your course. Keep Jack nice and round, and it will help you carry a nice smooth canter from fence to fence. I know I sound like a broken record when I say this to you, but it is really where you struggle, and if you can get it under control, you will see just how successful you can be."

Hearing the same thing over and over does take its toll on me, but Jayne is right. When I have him in a nice rhythm, we ride great. It is when he changes gaits unexpectedly, or even when he speeds up because I am asking him to, even though I don't really mean to, that I, as she likes to put it, "just stop riding." I almost turn off and decide at that moment that I can't control the situation and then Jack is the boss and can do what he wants out there.

For me a big part of what the last few weeks have been all about is getting more comfortable and confident with Jack's big canter stride, especially to fences. I need to be able to ride it comfortably to be successful, especially at places like WEC.

Knowing I don't have pressure to be ready for a show in the next couple of months allows me time to really focus on my riding. Between the training sessions I have with Jayne and our solo rides, I have put in a lot of extra time on those little things.

I am determined to have good outings at WEC, and it is coming up quickly. As of today, we leave in forty-five days.

FINAL COUNTDOWN

I check my calendar. In less than a month we head down to WEC for the week. Things are starting to feel more real now. Jack has his vet appointment this week for his microchip, and I have completed his USEF registration. Those items are a couple of the big ones on Jayne's to-do list that she gave to everyone.

"I was thinking about taking a trip to the tack store on Saturday. Want to go with me?" Hannah asks. "There are a few things that I still need to get for Fender, and I figured it would be something fun to do."

"Absolutely! I keep looking at this damn packet and all the things that I should probably already have for Jack, but I don't. Plus I need to wash his blankets, especially his stable sheet."

"Well at least you did his registration." Jayne laughs. "I keep telling Lana to get it done, but she pretty much is leaving everything up to me."

Equestrian Connection is our local tack store. It was a big deal when it opened about ten years ago, because there wasn't one close by at the time. Now we don't have to drive an hour to get the things we need. Ordering online may be convenient, but sometimes you need to see the items you are buying to make sure you are getting the right stuff.

"We should get lunch after we are finished spending a crazy amount of money on our horses. I think it'll make us feel better. I'm thinking a little lunch, maybe an adult beverage or two . . ." I shake my head. We like to joke about how much it costs to keep a horse, but honestly, the money is completely worth it. "We don't have to be at the barn to ride today, so it'll be nice. I feel like I have been at the barn every available hour of the day lately."

"Yeah, that sounds great."

We get to Equestrian Connection around noon. It isn't busy, which is nice. I have a decent-size list of things I need to get for Jack.

- *Poultice or green jelly—This is used for after we ride; it soothes the muscles in his legs.*
- *Horse treats—They stock his favorite, so I'll get some to take to WEC and keep in my locker at Schuster's.*

- *Riding gloves—My schooling ones are worn through, so I need to replace them.*
- *Perfect Prep—He will get this at WEC on show days, it helps keep him focused.*
- *Vet wrap—In case some random injury pops up. Plus, it is always good to have some on hand.*
- *White show breeches—The ones I own have several stains on them from use, so I figured now is the perfect time to buy a new pair.*
- *Tack cleaner—I go through a lot of it, so it is the perfect time to stock up on some.*

"Okay, I think I found most of the items on my list. I am going to just look around a bit to see if I missed anything."

Hannah and I spend about an hour in the tack store getting everything we need. What we didn't get we can order online and have delivered.

"Well, I've spent enough money here today. Let's get lunch. What are you in the mood for?"

"There is that really good burger place down the street, and they have the fall beer that I like on tap."

We grab our bags, put them in the car, and head to the restaurant.

"So it's getting pretty close to WEC. How are you feeling about things?"

"Ha! I think this is the craziest thing I have ever decided to do. Lana should be the only one showing Fender. There is no way that I can get out there in that arena and ride him." The look on Hannah's face is a combination of laughter and seriousness. She decided at the last minute that she did indeed want to go. Lana is home for Christmas break, so they will both get to ride.

"If I am getting out there, you are too. I can't do it alone. We'll ride our horses in the baby classes and let the younger girls do the big, fancy jumps. I am perfectly fine with that. Plus I just learned that my family isn't going because it is a far drive, so I will need the support."

My mom called me a few days ago to break the news that she wasn't going to make it to WEC after all. As much as she wanted to, the drive is just too much for her, and everyone else has to work. I tried to convince my older brother to take the time off. He still had three weeks before the show, but he said that it is their busy season, so any extra time off is not possible.

I understand, though. It's not like the venue is around the corner, but not having family there will make the experience seem less exciting. I really want to share it with them. I know they will be there in spirit and waiting for my phone call as soon as I finish riding, regardless of the outcome.

"I am sorry that they aren't coming. Your mom has never missed a show. You'll have us. You and me, us old ladies with all the young kids."

We both laugh, finish our lunch, and head home.

The last three weeks were a blur. It was a constant rotation of jump work and flat days, anything we could do in those last few moments to fine-tune our skills to get us ready for the big time. The entry fees are paid, the horses are vet checked and ready to go, and our bags are packed.

It was officially the final WEC countdown.

WE MADE IT

*F*inally it is here, the day we leave for WEC. It is Sunday morning, five a.m., and my alarm goes off. "Ugh! It can't possibly be time to get up already." The thought of having to wake up that early sounds miserable. I roll over, shut off the alarm, and sit up. "Today's the day." A small lump forms in the back of my throat. Part of me thought this trip wasn't actually going to happen, but here we are. We are all meeting up at the barn by six a.m. to make sure we have everything packed, although we've checked and rechecked it all about fifty times by now.

Four horses are going: Jack, Fender, Ruby, and Donatello, a horse that belongs to one of the other advanced junior riders. She also went to WEC last year.

It'll take us anywhere between three and four hours to drive down, depending on whether we need to stop on the way. Hannah, Lana, and I are driving together, and Lisa and Kristy, Donatello's owner, will also be driving together with their two girls. Luckily we are able to get all our stuff in the horse trailer and in two full-sized SUVs. I didn't realize how much stuff we were taking until it was all laid out in the aisles of the barn waiting to be packed up. I was glad about Jayne's packet and the list she made.

The drive down goes without a hitch. We arrive at the facility first. I tend to drive past the speed limit, and we didn't need to stop on the way.

"Holy shit!" That is my first reaction when we finally get there. "I knew it was big and fancy, but I wasn't expecting it to be quite so massive. Also, I've never been to anything like this before."

The grounds are absolutely gorgeous. With several barns, indoor and outdoor arenas, and plenty of turnout space, it really makes you feel special when you drive up.

"Yeah, this is really nice," I hear Lana say from the back seat.

Thanks to our registration packets that we received prior to leaving, we have a map of the grounds and know which barn our horses were going to be stabled in for the week. The directions on the property are laid out well, and we have no trouble finding our way around.

Once we have checked ourselves in at the show office, our first stop is to the stables. Our priority is always *horse first, then you,* especially when it is a new place and the horses are not familiar with things. Lisa and Kristy arrived only a few minutes after us. The seven of us together unload the trunks from the cars and start getting the stalls situated.

Jayne pulls in with the horses about a half an hour after we did, which gave us plenty of time to get the tack room set up and the stalls all bedded. It took us about two hours to get everything situated, including taking the horses for a walk around the facility. Next stop is the house we all rented. The house is only about a five-minute drive from the barn, which is perfect. We still have a lot of stuff to take out of the cars and none of us have eaten yet. Instead of cooking something, we decided to head out for lunch. We'd all come back to the barn and ride later, after the horses had been able to settle in.

Jayne posts a schedule for the week on each of our horse's stall doors. It includes information on feeding schedules, schooling ride times, and more importantly, our show schedules. We are all in different divisions, so it is important to know where we need to be and when. Unlike our local shows that will wait for you to make your way up to the ring, at rated shows if you aren't there on time, you miss out and don't show.

I have Jayne ride Jack our first time in the big arena. It isn't something I normally do, but I feel it is the best way to approach the show. She has no problem hopping on him first. In fact she almost insists. Being able to see how he is when she rides him puts me at ease. After about twenty minutes of her riding him around and sending him over a few of the jumps, I am ready to get on.

Our schooling session is the same as back home. Hannah and I together, and then Lana will take Fender over bigger fences when she schools with Ellie and Liz a little later. We begin with flat work, walk to trot to canter, and then move to over-fence work, starting with single fences to warm up. It is intimidating being in such a large space, but I try to ride like it is just any other lesson.

The two of us schooled for about an hour, working each fence individually and putting together small courses. The goal is not to overdo it or overwhelm us; we are doing that enough on our own. After we finish and the other girls warm up, Hannah and I stand in the center of the arena. "We made it, and we deserve to be here," I tell her, and we turn and walk out.

THE BIG TIME

*T*oday is our first day of showing, and when we arrive in the morning, the arena looks much bigger than it did the night before, during schooling.

The setup is beautiful, and I take Jack out to walk around the ring before the show officially starts. We have a couple of "I am not sure about this, Mom" moments, but he settles in nicely and has taken well to the atmosphere there.

Jayne ultimately decided to keep me in the two-foot division. I had the choice to go up to two feet, three inches, but since it was my first time doing any type of rated show, I felt it was better to stay where we were for most of the year, where we feel the most comfortable. We schooled over some of the bigger fences the previous night to get a little taste of what it would be like, but I was perfectly fine staying lower.

Since we are doing the two-foot division, that means I ride first. I am grateful that Hannah made the trip down also; she'll be in the class with us. Each class has about twenty or so riders, which makes placing extremely difficult. Good thing I don't dwell on the placings or winning ribbons. Jack and I are here for the experience, to get our first taste of rated showing. He is a big fancy horse; these are the types of shows he should be doing. He isn't going to win any confirmation awards by any means, but the way he moves and how he jumps, he grabs attention.

Our first hunter class is set for 9:30 Monday morning. The show officially kicks off at eight o'clock, so Jack and I will be in the second grouping of horses to go. Hannah and Fender drew the same group we did, which makes things a lot easier for Jayne and of course makes Hannah and me happy as well. We are also going to do Intro Jumpers while we are here, and that goes on later in the week, on Thursday.

I had already accepted that none of my family was going to be able to make it; they broke that news to me a couple of weeks earlier. I tried to understand. WEC is a decent drive from where we live, but it still makes it seem a little less important and a little less special without them here. I am lucky, though; the other moms are always support-ive and will make sure to take a lot of pictures and videos of us to commemorate the experience.

"Lou and Hannah, are your horses all tacked up and ready to go?" asked Jayne.

"Yeah, they just need bridling," we replied.

The show is well underway by now. They just announced group two to be ready to go in thirty minutes, which means we need to be warmed up and have our game faces on.

"Can you girls take Jack and Fender up to the ring while Hannah and Lou get their gloves and helmets on? I want to go over the course with them on the way."

Ellie takes Jack for me, and Liz takes Fender. Our ring is right by our stalls, so there is no rush. We have plenty of time to get there and still warm up.

"So here we are, don't be nervous. We rode this course yesterday. The horses are nice and relaxed. Don't think about the people in the crowd or the giant screens all lit up. If you go out there and ride like you do at home, you'll be perfect."

Pep talks complete, it is time to go. Of the two of us, I entered the ring first. I preferred it that way; get it over with. I am ready, as ready as I am going to be, anyway. Another ten minutes of warming up isn't going to change anything. Time to take the confidence I have built up and show.

"Now entering the ring for their first Adult Amateur 2' Hunter Rider Trip, Number 423 Whiskey Lullaby, ridden and owned by Louise Getz."

The way your name sounds over a PA system is everything an equestrian dreams of. It resonates through the arena, and I feel like an Olympian out there.

The jumps are beautiful, brick and stone walls, greenery around the poles, and poinsettias everywhere, like a winter wonderland. All we need to get through the first course is eight fences, a couple of single fences, a diagonal line, a roll-back turn, and an outside line. Nothing we haven't practiced a thousand times.

We miss our distance on the first fence, I chip in, falling slightly forward on Jack's neck. He doesn't react. I sit up, regroup, and keep pushing forward. We found our rhythm again and hit the next fence perfectly.

"Remember to breathe" is all I can hear from Jayne as we pass the gate coming off our first fence.

I exhale. "Good boy, Jack, we can do this," and without even thinking, those two small gestures change everything, and we both settle in.

The outside line is the judge's line, which is where you really want to be perfect, show off what you and your horse can do. It is set as a five stride, but we couldn't hit that during schooling the previous night. Today is different. Jack is nice and forward, and when we jump the in fence, I know we have it. A perfect five strides and then the out fence. Nothing chipped, nothing rushed, perfect. We end our run with the traditional courtesy circle and exit the ring.

After we finish, we walk around the warmup ring waiting to return for our next course. I use this moment to take it all in, to allow myself a quick second of self-appreciation. I don't do it enough.

The stands are fairly crowded, but I manage to find our barn, and to my surprise, there they are, all of them: my mom (of course she found a way to be here; I don't know why I even doubted for a second that she wouldn't make it), my dad, my niece who took the day off of school to be here, both my brothers, and the friends that say they're coming but never actually do. They are here also. I have my own little cheering section, and when they spot me, they all stand up and wave. It is hard to hold back the tears.

Jayne makes her way over to talk with me about our ride. "Everything okay? You looked great out there. A little miscommunication at the beginning, but that was it. Everything else was exactly how we practiced it; you even got the five strides in the outside line."

"Oh yeah, I am super pleased with our ride, right, Jack?" I give him a pat on the head. "Did you know they were here?" I point to where everyone is in the stands.

"I did, yes. Your mom talked to me about it last week during your niece's lesson. She wanted to make sure she knew when you were riding and what time they needed to be here. She wasn't going to miss it, but she made me promise not to tell you. She wanted it to be a surprise."

I have two more jumping rounds and some flat classes still to get through this morning, so I wipe my tears, take a drink of water, and head back to the ring for my next round.

The rest of the division take their turns, including Hannah and Fender. That was it for us for the day. Later we would watch Ellie, Lana, and Liz ride, which is how the week would go, us and then them. At night we would have dinner together and do one last check on our horses.

Thursday, after we finished with jumpers, we would casually start getting everything packed up. First thing Friday morning we would head home.

REACHING NEW HEIGHTS

*O*ur week at WEC was fulfilling. Jack and I managed to bring home a couple of ribbons, two sixth places, one seventh place, and even fifth place in one of our jumper classes. It was an exhilarating experience, and having my family and friends surprise me and make the trip down to support us was a delight. We took a lot of pictures to commemorate the trip, and I even bought some professional ones. In a few we looked super fancy, and I couldn't resist.

That was it, the year is over, nothing to work toward for a while, just our normal lessons and training schedule. I really enjoy showing, but I also think that taking a break after a long show season or even just an intense week of showing is especially important for both you and your horse. It gives you a chance to wind down and recover. It also gives you the opportunity to think about what's next, a new concept for me. *Next* used to mean "When I sell Jack and get another horse, we can talk about what comes next." The fact that next now means moving up a division or two this upcoming show season, and going to more rated or even some dressage shows is the icing on my adult amateur's cake.

Riding horses can take a toll on you, both mentally and physically. Let's face it; it is a demanding sport. It is the only sport where men and women compete against each other at the same level, which is fascinating because we are separated in basketball, tennis, and swimming, even our counterpart to baseball, softball, is different. Every other sport has a women's team and a men's team. It doesn't mean we are any less talented, athletic, or committed to playing. You get a different feeling with equestrian sports. Knowing you'll compete against the best regardless of gender is cool.

Where do Jack and I go now? If you had asked me at the beginning of the year, the answer wouldn't have been positive. In fact I am not certain I would have even had an answer to give, but after this rewarding year of rediscovery and growth the answer is simple: *More*, we are going to continue to do more. My ultimate dream, regardless of the horse, has always been to show at the Kentucky

Horse Park. The difference now is that I have Jack and he has me. We are a team and turning into a pretty darn good one. The Kentucky Horse Park is the epitome of show venues for this part of the country, and getting to ride at that facility would be the ultimate "We did it, Jack!" moment.

Jack was a scrawny, underweight, off-the track Thoroughbred baby when I bought him. He had a crazy mohawk and terrible skin. Jack today is a gorgeous seventeen-hand, deep chestnut Thoroughbred athlete. And I am the same adult amateur equestrian who through many trials and tribulations, during which I was always proud to call him mine, has finally found her stride with her horse. Now we are riding high and reaching new heights together.

EPILOGUE

The winter season has been nice and relaxing for Jack and me. We've spent most of our time at Schuster's continuing to improve and get ready for the upcoming spring show season. We have begun taking lessons with Hannah and Fender, which has been a very positive experience for both of us. I need to work on building more confidence with group lessons.

Jack has been officially cleared by the vet, no longer requiring any type of medication for EPM. My niece joined me at my barn and even started riding Jack a little bit. Watching the two of them is the ultimate aunt moment.

Jayne's other riders, Ellie and Liz, decided to continue showing in the winter circuit with Ruby and Donatello, bringing home impressive awards each time.

We have also had the pleasure of participating

in several jumping and dressage clinics over the winter. I have always enjoyed clinics; they allow you to step out of your comfort zone and get feedback from different trainers.

I still dream of going to the Kentucky Horse Park one day with Jack, and who knows if it is in the cards for us? We'll just have to wait and see, but what I can say is that there are many more shows and adventures in store for us.

ABOUT THE AUTHOR

Alexis Minnich is an adult amateur equestrian who lives in Northeast Ohio. She has been riding horses for more than twenty years and has a passion for Thoroughbreds. She has a love for animals, sports, and spending time with her family. *Amateur Dreams* is her debut novel and was written as a thank you to those in her life who helped make her horseback riding dreams a reality.

Printed in the USA
CPSIA information can be obtained
at www.ICGtesting.com
JSHW082125061123
51321JS00009B/99